Rory's Rainbow

Written & Illustrated by

Melissa Piva

This book is dedicated to Nate, Mikey & Joyce –
You are each exactly who you are meant to be, and I will always
love you exactly as you are.

Love Mom

xo

MESSAGE TO READERS

The story Rory's Rainbow was written in hopes of promoting acceptance and inclusion. It is meant to send the message to children that acceptance should be unconditional. This story features characters that are gender non-conforming, and uses singular they as their pronouns. This was done not only to encourage use of gender non-specific pronouns, but also to keep the story more widely relatable for readers. Thank you for your support.

ACKNOWLEDGMENTS

I would like to extend a big Thank You to the following people for their support of my Rory's Rainbow Indiegogo campaign: Nicole Goetz, Claire & Jordyn Elliott, Karen Rockwell, Carly Cookson, Karen Kilbride, William Vigneux, Maureen Byrne, Sandra Rowe, Jon Cross, Bonnie Deslippe, Anna, Nancy Bauer, Ruth Barcus & Valerie Johnson.

I also want to express a huge Thank You to all my family and my friends. For believing in me, supporting me, helping with edits and revisions, telling me that I'm awesome when I have my doubts, and for being the amazing, accepting and wonderful people that you are. The world needs more people like all of you! Thank You! xo

Rory lived in a toy store.

To be specific, Rory lived on the third shelf from the floor in the boys' toys section of Tulso's Toy Store on Wondermore Street.

Rory was a lot like the other dinosaurs in the toy store –

They were all filled with soft cotton stuffing, they each had a long tail, and they all stood exactly the same height. (16 inches to be precise.)

And all of the dinosaurs at Tulso's Toy Store were the same shade of bright green as a fresh Spring leaf.

But deep inside –

Rory felt different.

While the other dinosaurs were happy in the
boys' section of the store, surrounded by the
cool blue hot rod cars and green army men,
Rory felt out of place.

Rory liked a whole rainbow of colours. They liked the bright red and yellow of the inflatable beach balls, and the vibrant orange of the plush clown fish.

But most of all, Rory liked the bright, cheerful colours that they could see across the room on the shelves that held the girls' toys.

Each night after the toy store closed Rory would slip down off the third shelf from the floor in the boys' toys section, inch past the building blocks and puzzles, and sneak just close enough to see the girls' toys section.

From there in their hiding spot Rory took in sites that filled them with joy.

Rory could see the pretty dolls dancing in their bright pink dresses.

They could watch the plush purple bears playing dress up in the colourful costumes.

And Rory would watch as they gathered together at the end of the night for a fancy tea party, using the tiniest of toy tea cups.

Oh, how Rory wished to join them! It looked like so much fun!

It was late one evening, as Rory was watching from behind a toy bowling set, when the beautiful doll suddenly stopped dancing. Something had caught her eye.

She was looking right at Rory, and waving!

The doll invited Rory to come out and play
in the girls' toys section.

Rory was delighted!

How thrilling it was to finally be able to put on a tutu and dance with the beautiful doll!

And how exciting to be able to dress up in beautiful costumes with the purple bears!

Rory even stayed to drink the pretend tea
from the tiny toy tea cups at the tea party!

Rory was so happy and was having so much fun that they completely lost track of time until it was very, very late at night.

They were so tired that with a smile upon their face and surrounded by wonderful, new friends, they fell sound asleep in the girls' toys section.

In the morning Rory woke to the sound of keys and footsteps as Mr. Tulso unlocked the front door and entered the store, his youngest grandchild trailing behind him.

Realizing that they hadn't made it back to the shelf with all the other dinosaurs, or taken off the tutu, Rory panicked. They were still in the girls' toys section.

Caught up in thoughts of how to sneak back without being seen, Rory didn't realize that Mr. Tulso's grandchild had approached the shelf and was regarding them with a curious expression.

A small hand picked up Rory. Mr. Tulso's grandchild looked at the dinosaur in the soft, pink tutu, and then embraced them.

"You're just like me!" they whispered. Rory was filled with happiness.

"What have you got there, Riley?" asked Mr. Tulso walking up behind them. "Oh, that's a dinosaur! That belongs in the boys' toys," he said, reaching for Rory.

"No, Grandpa," said Riley. "They are like me. They belong here. Look at their tutu. Look at their smile! This dinosaur is like me!"

Mr. Tulso looked at Riley a bit puzzled for a moment, and then he looked around his store. He looked at the wall of boys' toys at one end of the store. Then he looked at the wall of girls' toys at the other end of the store.

"You know what, Riley?" Mr. Tulso exclaimed. "I think you're right. And, I have an important job that I could use your help with today."

That day Rory watched from the counter as Mr. Tulso and Riley re-arranged the toy store.

Mr. Tulso put the soccer balls next to the pink roller skates. Riley moved the model airplanes so they were next to pretty ponies. And then they put the leafy green dinosaurs beside the dancing dolls in the bright pink dresses.

When they were finished Mr. Tulso's toy store was a colourful rainbow of fun. The toys were no longer divided into boys' and girls' sections.

Rory had never felt so happy, and neither had Riley. Finally, they both felt like they had somewhere that they belonged.

A message to anyone reading this book & anyone who just needs to hear it –

You are important. You matter. You deserve to be loved and accepted just as you are. Never change to try to make anyone happy – unless it's yourself. Don't ever give up.

xo

Made in the USA
Columbia, SC
31 March 2022